Spike the Dhog

Enjoy!
Annie Gifford
Priscilla Gifford

Written by Priscilla Gifford
Illustrated by Anne Gifford

Especially for
SOPHIE~
Happy Reading!

Spike
the Dhog

Written by Priscilla Gifford
Illustrated by Anne Gifford

Thank you to Tracy Rowland, Linda Parks, Ann Hayes, Harriet Peck Taylor, Kathy Sievering, Janet Stevens, Bruce Iden, Joan Cheng and so many others for all of their help, inspiration and support.

Thank you to my son, Lexis Telischak, for creating Mr. Moon.

One quiet October night,
Spike the Dhog
fell out of the sky like a shooting star.

He had little pink pig eyes, a thick row of
hedgehog hair, and a tail that pointed backwards
to show where he had been.

He landed with a loud PLOP, all alone in a field near a winding stream. Spike gazed up into the sky at the friendly moon.

Mr. Moon looked at Spike's pig parts, and he looked at Spike's hedgehog parts. At last he spoke.

"Well, I think you are a very special kind of animal.
You seem to be a little bit of pig,
and a tiny bit of hedgehog,
but you act like a dog.
I will name you a....Dhog!"

Spike asked, "Mr. Moon, I am looking for
a happy home. Where shall I go?"
Mr. Moon told him, "Just follow that stream."

"Thank you", said Spike, who started walking
on his sturdy legs over the lumpy field.

As Spike the Dhog walked, he brushed against a tall prickly plant
with pink fuzzy flowers. "Ouch," he cried.
"Those leaves are as sharp as my hair!"
A small brown face poked out of a hole in the ground and asked,
"Who are you?" It was a prairie dog.

"Oh, hi, I'm Spike the Dhog,
and I'm looking for a home.
May I stay with you?"

"My, you are a strange looking dog,
but we would be happy to have you",
answered the prairie dog.

"Why, thank you" replied Spike.
He tried to wriggle down the snug hole
but poor Spike was too chubby.
"I guess I'll have to find a home that fits me.
So long, fellows."

Spike the Dhog kept on walking beside the bubbling water.
He paused on a wooden bridge and looked down.
Suddenly, a big fish jumped out of the stream.
Spike said quickly, "Hi, I'm Spike the Dhog
and I'm looking for a home. May I stay with you?"

"My," the fish answered,
"you are a strange looking dog,
but come join me, the water's fine!"

Spike smiled happily. He leaped into the cold water.
He sank to the bottom like a rock. Spike could not swim!
He gasped for air as he scrambled up the grassy bank.
He shook himself dry. "Sorry," he told the fish.
"I guess I'll have to find a drier home."

Soon Spike the Dhog came nose-to-nose with a turtle and asked,
"Hi, I'm Spike the Dhog, and I'm looking for a home.
May I stay with you?"

"My, you are a strange looking dog," said the turtle. "This shell is my home, but there is only enough room inside for me. Sorry!"

"I guess I'll have to find a home that has room for me," Spike told the turtle.

Spike continued on his way. He saw a black and white bird flying overhead. It was a magpie. Spike flapped his front legs as fast as he could, but he didn't even lift off the ground.

Spike ran along, following the bird until it landed.
"Hi, I'm Spike the Dhog, and I'm looking for a home.
May I stay with you?"

"My, you are a strange looking dog.
What kind of an animal are you, anyway?
Can you fly to our nest?
You don't have any wings," teased the birds.

Spike felt too sad to answer the unkind magpies.
"I guess I'll have to find a home that is closer to the ground,"
he said to himself. He saw a red barn in the valley below.
Spike put on his bravest smile
and marched across the field toward the farm.

The barnyard was full of plump cats.
Spike wagged his tail and said,
"Hi, I'm Spike the Dhog and I'm looking for a home.
May I stay with you?"

"My, you are a strange looking dog,"
hissed their leader.

Spike was afraid of these cats! "Hisssss…..hisssss….
dogs are not welcome in our barn. Hissssss…hisssss….hissssss."
"I guess I'll have to find a home that isn't so scary," said Spike.
He slinked behind the barn with his tail between his legs.

Some pigs were there, eating busily.
"Hi, I'm Spike the Dhog and I'm looking for a home.
May I stay with you?"

"My, you are a strange looking dog,"
grunted a pig.

"Look at your snout! You seem a little bit like us,
but your nose is so funny."

One pig started to laugh, and then another,
until all of them were giggling and pointing at Spike.

They grew louder, and LOUDER, and LOUDER!
Spike knew that he could not find a happy home
with these pestering pigs.

"I guess I'll have to find a home that isn't so noisy,"
he said as he hurried away.

Spike the Dhog trudged along the dirt road into the cool forest. He stopped to rest under a tall green tree.

"Hi, I'm Spike the Dhog and I'm looking for a home. May I stay with you?" he asked.

The silent tree did not answer, so Spike walked on.

Soon he came upon a mama bear and her baby cub. "Hi, I'm Spike the Dhog and I'm looking for a home. May I stay with you?" he pleaded.

"My, you are a strange looking dog," answered the bear.
"We are about to crawl into our cozy den to sleep until spring."
"That's too much sleeping for me," Spike told the bear.
"I guess I'll have to find a home where I won't have to be so quiet."

Spike was hungry and tired.
He nibbled on some berries and lay down
under a bush to rest.

"Maybe I'll just live alone right here,"
he told himself sadly.

After a little nap, Spike felt better.
He crept from the bushes and began to walk
toward a town at the edge of the forest.

Spike soon found himself on a busy bicycle path.
Everyone was zipping by in such a rush!
Where were they going?

He tried to get their attention.
"Hi, I'm Spike the Dhog and I'm looking for a home.
May I stay with you?" he asked.
Nobody noticed him.

He heard wheels spinning, bells ringing,
and gears shifting.
Did anyone even see him?

Spike crawled into the bushes by the side of the path.
A tear rolled down his freckled cheek.
It was really hard to find a home.

Suddenly, Spike heard a swirling, whooshing noise
from somewhere up in the sky. His pointy ears perked up.

And then, KAPLUMP!
Something crashed down near him.
It was made of thin sticks and heavy, brightly colored paper.
A house!
Spike squealed as he crawled under it.

He heard a girl's voice from across the grass.
Spike stood up quickly.
His sharp hair poked through the paper.
He scurried toward the voice.

"Where's my kite? There it is. Look! It's walking!"
All that the girl could see was part of a nose and a pointy tail
peeking out from under her crumpled kite.
She ran towards Spike.

The girl plucked her kite from Spike's prickly hair.
Spike put on his best smile and said,
"Hi, I'm Spike the Dhog, and I'm looking for a home.
May I stay with you?"

The girl hugged Spike.
"I don't know what kind of animal you are, but I like your pointy ears,
your round fuzzy nose, your little pig hooves, your bristly hair,
and most of all, your happy smile. I like every bit of you!"

The girl picked up her wrinkled kite.

"I will make a perfect home for you," she told Spike.
"Follow me."

The cozy house that she built in her yard was just the right size.
It wasn't too small, too wet, too high, too scary, too noisy, or too quiet.
At last Spike had found a home of his own and someone to love him.
He lay down inside to dream happy Dhog dreams.
Up in the sky, Mr. Moon smiled down on Spike the Dhog.

The End

Made in the USA
Charleston, SC
26 September 2014